When
Winter
Robeson
Came

When Winter Robeson Came

Brenda Woods

◎ NANCY PAULSEN BOOKS

NANCY PAULSEN BOOKS
An imprint of Penguin Random House LLC, New York

First published in the United States of America by Nancy Paulsen Books,
an imprint of Penguin Random House LLC, 2022

Visit us online at penguinrandomhouse.com

Library of Congress Cataloging-in-Publication Data
Names: Woods, Brenda (Brenda A.) author.
Title: When Winter Robeson came / Brenda Woods.
Description: New York: Nancy Paulsen Books, [2022] | Summary: In August 1965, twelve-year-old
Eden's older cousin from Mississippi comes to visit her in Los Angeles, and while the Watts Riots erupt
around them, they continue their investigation of the disappearance of Winter's father ten years ago.
Identifiers: LCCN 2021032566 | ISBN 9781524741587 (hardcover) |
ISBN 9781524741594 (ebook)
Subjects: CYAC: Novels in verse. | Cousins—Fiction. | Fathers and sons—Fiction. |
African Americans—Fiction. | Race relations—Fiction. | Watts Riot, Los Angeles, Calif., 1965—Fiction.
| Los Angeles (Calif.)—Fiction. | LCGFT: Novels in verse.
Classification: LCC PZ7.5.W665 Wh 2022 | DDC [Fic]—dc23
LC record available at https://lccn.loc.gov/2021032566

Book manufactured in Canada

ISBN 9781524741587
1 3 5 7 9 10 8 6 4 2
FRI

Design by Eileen Savage | Text set in Maxime Std

In loving memory of Jessica L. Brown

All God's angels come to us disguised.

—*James Russell Lowell*

When
Winter
Robeson
Came

Unexpected Endings

When my cousin, Winter Robeson, came, I figured
it would simply be two weeks of summertime fun.
But every now and then it seems like songs with
    unexpected endings:
Things don't always turn out the way you thought
    they would.
August 1965 wound up becoming
exactly like one of those songs.

A Volcano Erupts

The melody began harmoniously.

Instantly, Winter and I became a duo; our ballad, a duet.

But it wasn't long before the tempo of our song changed.

Poco a poco—little by little—the music veered off course,

becoming an improvisation: spontaneous, unrehearsed.

Then, suddenly and without warning, the city of Watts,

which people claim was a volcano aching to erupt,

finally did.

Free-Flowing Melodies

Eden, Eden Louise Coal, is my name.
I'm twelve, going on thirteen.
I live on 103rd Street in Los Angeles, California,
just west of Figueroa, not too far from Watts.
Something else I suppose you should know
is that I plan to become a songwriter, and so
my words often pour out in cascading streams,
sounding like free-flowing melodies.

His Arrival

It's a summertime Thursday, August 5, 1965.
We're downtown at Union Station, Daddy and I,
sitting inside on one of the long, cool wooden benches,
    waiting.
Now and then a train unloads, and passengers stream out.
Hands begin waving, and people hurry toward each other,
smiling, reaching out arms, hugging, sometimes kissing.
His train arrives late, but then there *he* is.
All the way from Sunflower, Mississippi,
birthplace of Jerry Butler, Daddy likes to brag.
Been two years since I last saw him
at our family reunion in Indianola, Miss.
I glance up at him, thinking, He sure grew tall,
and that makes me feel small.
He'll be fourteen this December,
our cousin, Winter Robeson.

I'm Eden, I blurt.

I know. You ain't changed 'cept you got a lot shorter, Winter
    Robeson jokes.

I laugh. *Did not,* I tell him, then examine him from head to toe.

The straw cowboy hat looks small for his head,

and for some reason that makes me smile.

Between his front teeth a gap has appeared,

and his perfect velvety skin is dark brown.

His suitcase Mama would call well used.

His plaid shirt is green; his jeans, brand-new blue.

His black high-top Converses have snowy-white laces,

and from his neck a Kodak camera loosely dangles.

We trail my daddy, Ernie Coal, outside into the sun.

From the front seat of our '57 Chevy, I keep turning
    around, gazing,

sipping him slowly like ice water, memorizing him
    like a poem.

Y'all even have your own automobile. Wish we had one,
    Winter remarks,

caressing the seat, acting like he's riding in a fancy
    Cadillac Coupe de Ville.

I turn on the radio, and music fills the car.

Marvin Gaye is singing "I'll Be Doggone," and I sing along.

Immediately, Winter joins in, and together we croon.

When the song ends, Winter begins snapping pictures.

Click, click, click.

California, he softly says, making it sound like heaven.

It gets in your blood after 'while, Daddy confesses.

Not like Mississippi, but it does.

And right then, once again, I begin to long

for the country roads and folks of Indianola, Mississippi,

where I was born and raised till I was ten.

Missing Her and Mississippi

Mississippi,
where trios of songbirds serenaded me in the morning
and lightning bugs added sparkle to summertime nights.

Mississippi,
where I spent Sundays singing old-time hymns
in our tiny white wooden church with the pipe organ,
and Saturdays taking piano lessons from Miss Elvira Porter.

Miss Elvira Porter, her hands wrinkled but fingers
    still nimble,
taught me how to read notes and play,
plus musical symbols and terms galore.
I'm not sure if she planted the seed of music in me
or if it was already there, just waiting for her to cultivate.

From her creaky porch swing, where she and I loved
    to linger,
she spoke of Negro women composers,
like Margaret Bonds and Julia Perry,
writers of spirituals, sonatas, symphonies, even operas,
and trained me to hear life's orchestra.
Hear that, Eden? she asked.

Hear what?

The whip-poor-wills singing, the dog barking in the distance,
the gentle breeze rustling the leaves of the cypress trees.
Now the train, hear it rolling along the tracks?
Getting louder . . . crescendo . . . shh, softer now . . . decrescendo.
There's the train's conductor, his horn a-blowing.
Finally, the climax, my teakettle inside, whistling.
It's a beautiful composition, wouldn't you say?
I would, yes, ma'am, I would.

Missing her and Mississippi makes me sigh.

And I ache for it even more with Winter nearby.

The tone of his voice, the warmth of his smile,
    bring me back.

And for the thousandth time, I wish we'd never left.

103rd Street

Our house looks pretty with its square patch of emerald-
    green lawn, freshly mowed.
Pink geraniums are blooming, and the picture window is
    Windex clean.
Inside, everything is what my daddy calls spick-and-span,
and Mama has fixed things up especially nice,
the way she always does for visits from folks back home.
It's like Mama's bound and determined to wash off her
    country beginnings as if they're a stain
    and a life in California is a fancy detergent,
guaranteed to get rid of it, once and for all.

Mama steps onto the front porch.
Her lipstick is red; hair freshly pressed and curled;
green-and-white polka-dot sundress starched and perfect.
Grinning and waving, she rushes to the car,
my mama, Ruby Coal.

Mama hugs Winter so tightly that a laugh pops up
  out of him.

As handsome as your daddy, J.T., she says, her voice sounding
  sweet—dolce.

I notice that Mama's mention of his daddy, who disappeared
and is likely dead, changes Winter's eyes from happy to sad.

Yet still, he politely replies, *Thank you, Miz Ruby.*

It's so nice to have you here, Winter, Mama tells him.

His face brightens, and again he says, *Thank you, Miz Ruby.*

It's most kind of y'all to have me.

The Gum Smacker

The next-door neighbor's screen door opens,
its usual squeal turning our attention its way.
Hi, Mr. and Miz Coal . . . and Eden, she adds reluctantly,
as if I'm insignificant, the way she always does,
gum-smacking fifteen-year-old
   thinks-she's-a-Hollywood-movie-star
Cassie Webber.

Mama and Daddy give a courteous reply and head inside.
Then Cassie Webber blows a huge, perfect pink bubble,
   pops it with her finger,
and stares at my cousin, Winter,
as if he's a blinking neon sign.
Who are you? she asks.

I'm Eden's cousin, Winter.
Did you say "Winter"?

Yes, I did, he tells her.

What kind of a name is that?

The one my daddy gave me, born the first day of winter is why.

Oh, she says. *That's strange but kinda cool.*

And as she gazes at Winter,

I swear I see stars in the gum smacker's eyes.

As we make our escape, Winter confides, *She's just sayin'*
what most folks think 'bout my name being strange. I mean,
even my buddies poke fun and tease,
"Put your coats on, y'all, 'cuz Winter's comin' and I feel a breeze."
I smile and so does he.

The Sophisticated Metropolis

Have a seat, young man, Daddy tells him.
After such a long trip, you must be tired.
Winter plops and glances around.
Thissa real nice place y'all have here.
Mama fidgets with her copper beads, grins,
   and proudly says,
It's called California Modern style. I decorated it myself.
Never seen nuthin' like this in Sunflower, Winter comments.
Mama plumps a pillow. *Of course not, Winter.*
Los Angeles is a sophisticated metropolis.

Cooking food has warmed the house, and the aromas lure
   me to the kitchen.
One by one, I lift the lids and inhale.
It's not Sunday, but even so, a Sunday supper is on its way.
Green beans and ham hocks; potatoes buttered and mashed;
short ribs bubbling in brown gravy.

Inside the oven, cornbread bakes.

Since we moved to Los Angeles, a lot of things have
    changed.

But our suppertime meals, the kind that make
    my mouth water,

have thankfully stayed the same.

The Itinerary

I sit opposite Winter and start to chatter, my tempo
   lively—vivace.
One day, if you like, we'll go to Sportsman Park to swim in
   the indoor pool.
But if you like the movies, and who doesn't, there's
   the Rio Theatre, the Imperial,
and the Manchester, too, and—
Winter interrupts. *Is Watts far from here?*
Not too far, I answer. *Why?*
Just wondering, he replies.

I continue jabbering,
Saturday night we're going to a mostly-for-grown-ups party
at my best friend Winona's, who used to live around the corner.
Just last month they moved to a house up in Baldwin Hills.
It's two stories and even has a swimming pool.
Now Mama wants to move there, too,
but Daddy says 103rd Street is fine with him.

I rattle on,

Sunday after church we're going to Playa del Rey Beach.

And all day next Saturday is reserved for Disneyland.

Mama and I wrote it down. It's called an itinerary.

If you never heard that word, it means "travel plan."

Mama made me look it up.

Mama adds,

For some culture, the museums and rose garden at Exposition
Park are a quick bus ride down Figueroa.

Daddy lets out a powerful laugh.

That's enough, you two. Let the young man catch his breath.

He'll be here two whole weeks. There's plenty of time.

Winter guzzles the last of his soda, then all he says is,

Plenty of time? I sure hope so.

The Motive

My eyes don't want to open, but the *Boing! Boing! Boing!*
sound that woke me keeps going and going.
Maurice Webber, Cassie's younger brother,
on his beloved pogo stick in their driveway next door.

I glance at my clock. It's barely seven.
Doesn't he know summertime mornings are for sleeping?
I fold the pillow over my head, trying to muffle the sound.
Finally, he stops, and quickly, I drift back to sleep.
Then, *Boing! Boing! Boing!* He's at it again.
Having little choice, I let the noisemaker win,
and lazily crawl out of bed.

From the front window, I peek.
The car's gone, meaning Daddy's left for work.
Mama has the day off and is probably still asleep.

Across the street, old Mr. Fitzpatrick, who Daddy and
   Mama call Fitz,
picks up his newspaper and scans the block
as his dog, Fred, runs circles around his feet.

Boing! Boing! Boing! Maurice starts up again.
I swing open the side window. *Maurice!* I shout. *Stoppit!*
You can't make me, Eden!
Boing! Boing! Boing!
Right then, Winter shuffles in, rubbing his sleepy eyes.
What's that sound?
I point at Maurice. *Pogo stick.*
Winter yells, *Can I try?*
The noisemaker smiles and tells him, *Sure.*

And that's how we wind up outside in our pajamas,
Winter bouncing here and there, trying hard to keep
   his balance,
sometimes succeeding, other times failing,
until Mama sticks her face out the window.
Why are you two outside in your pajamas?
Pogo stick, I explain. *Winter's learning.*
C'mon in the house, both of you, waking up the world.

Winter grins. *But it's fun, Miz Ruby.*
You hear me? Mama fusses.

We are heading inside when, for the second time,
Winter asks, *How far is Watts from here?*
I told you yesterday, not that far.
Too far to walk?
We could, but the bus is quicker. You wanna see the Towers,
    huh?
Towers?
The Watts Towers. They're cool!
This man named Simon built them totally by himself,
but once people see, they find that hard to believe.
The towers are the usual reason why folks who come to visit us
want to go to Watts . . . unless they have family there.
Winter's gaze turns sad—mesto—and he says,
It's where my daddy lived before he disappeared.
All of a sudden it becomes crystal clear, and I know.
Winter didn't come here for Disneyland, Hollywood, or
    the beach.
I peer into his eyes. *You came here looking for your daddy,*
    huh?
His nod confirms my belief.

I know it's been almost ten years, but there's just gotta be someone who remembers him, a trail he left somewhere.

I nod in agreement. *Want Mama and Daddy to help?*

No, just wanna snoop around by myself.

I'm a good snoop, I tell him. *Can I come along?*

Sure. Plus, you know this city.

Yeah, I sorta do.

For now, can it be our secret, Eden?

I reply, *It can.*

Secrets

For breakfast we have eggs, sunny-side up, bacon and grits,
and glasses of ice-cold milk.
Daddy claims keeping a secret, good or bad, makes you
    uncomfortable.
And that must be true, because Winter's way more at ease.
But now that I've promised his secret to keep, I'm feeling a
    little bit fidgety
and knock over my glass, spilling the milk.

Doubts and Lists

Mama asks, *Eden Louise? Did you practice your music*
 yesterday?
I lie, *Yes, ma'am, I did.*
Winter's face lights up. *You play an instrument?*
The piano.
His eyes scan the room.
In the garage, I explain. *I usually take lessons once a week,*
except now I'm off for the summer.

Fact is, California was slowly wilting the musical dreams
Miss Elvira Porter had begun to nourish.
My teacher here came highly recommended.
Mr. Marcus Antonius Duvall, brimming with
 musical expertise,
but with a love of it missing from his soul.
When I professed my desire to compose music,
an opera even, like *Porgy and Bess,* he shook his head.

But you're a girl, Miss Coal.

And to that, I replied, *I know.*

The seed of doubt sown, I hadn't practiced since.

Can you even read music? Winter asks.

I nod yes, and he replies,

Learn to read music, that's on my list.

List, what kind of list?

Winter Robeson's Lifetime List of Things to Do, he tells me.

What else is on your list?

So far, 123 things . . .

Mama interrupts,

As soon as you two finish, do the dishes.

Then get dressed and put on decent clothes.

Today's itinerary is the art museum.

I glance at my cousin. *Museum? Do we have to?*

Can we please go to the Watts Towers instead? I beg.

Not today. But you two can go there tomorrow.

I have my church meeting, and your daddy has to work half day.

You don't mind going by yourselves, do you?

Winter and I lock eyes and grin.

A Sour Memory

Friday, August 6, 1965, we walk outside into a not-hot
    summertime day.
Cassie is out dancing on her porch. As usual, her transistor
    radio is turned up too loud,
and she's singing along way off-key.
Would someone please tell that girl she can't sing?
Mama says playfully as she locks the front door.
You can't sing! Winter hollers.

Now we have her full attention.
She turns down the radio. *Huh?*
Shhh, Mama tells him.
But Winter disagrees. *Folks who can't sing oughta be told,*
    Miz Ruby.
No point in pretending.
I double over, laughing.
Be kind, Mama warns.

You're the one who said she can't sing, Mama.
Ruby Coal defends herself: *But I didn't announce it*
  to the neighborhood.
Still.
Are you getting fresh, Eden Louise?
I am, but I reply, *No, ma'am.*

Hi! Cassie calls out as we walk past, her eyes, like before,
  focused on Winter.
We say hello, wave goodbye, and head to the bus stop.

As we walk, I wish I could turn today into tomorrow
and that Winter and I were already snooping around
about his disappeared daddy's whereabouts.
I want to talk about it, but because Mama's with us, I can't,
  and it's hard.
Keeping my lip buttoned usually is.

And as we climb aboard, Winter notes, *Y'all never had to sit*
  in the back of the bus out here, huh?
No, no back of the bus, Mama echoes, *unless that's where you*
  choose to sit.
Winter parks himself right behind the driver and says,

I know the law says Jim Crow is supposed to be over and all,
but back home, so as not to cause trouble,
most of us, including me, still sit in the back.
He pauses, looks over the bus, and declares,
Being able to sit where you please, without being afraid,
*   feels mighty good.*
It sure does. I suppose two years of living in California
has nearly robbed me of that sour memory.
Silently, I remember and think, if I were to write a song
    about it,
I would name it just that, "A Sour Memory."

The Orchestra of Los Angeles

Downtown—cars honking, buses weaving, people dashing.
We wait for the next bus, and before long, it scoops us up.
It's crowded, forcing us to stand and steady ourselves
each time the driver stops, then starts.
Y'all like it here, in California? Winter asks as we chug along.
Mama immediately answers, *Yes indeed.*
But I shrug. *Some days I do, but mostly I miss the country and
    quiet.*

For Ruby Coal, this sophisticated metropolis is clearly
    the winner.
Unlike me, she feels no tug-of-war with Mississippi.
I daydream, and my thoughts wander back to Indianola.
I miss its music, often picked on four-string banjos,
accompanied by tambourines and harmonicas
that invited me to sway and hum along.

Indianola, Mississippi, where so many knew me by name.
And I wasn't just Eden; I was Eden Louise.
You hurry on home now, Eden Louise.
It's gettin' near dusk, child, they'd warn,
their voices filled with concern for my safety as if they were
  kin to me.
Carry this bag of turnips to your mama, Eden Louise,
and some freshly churned butter too.
Their smiles held the sun and the moon.

To me, Los Angeles is like a full orchestra,
alive with instruments, minus the harmony.
Airplanes roaring above, cars honking, tires screeching,
the wail of fire engines and police car sirens,
music from a neighbor's stereo, way after midnight,
then, thankfully, some quiet.

At the museum, Winter waves a make-believe paintbrush
as we stand in front of a Picasso.
I like to make art instead of looking at it.
Are you any good? Mama asks.
Art teacher insists I am.
An artiste, Mama says in a fancy way.

Fitz

We make our way back home. Mr. Fitzpatrick greets us,
and his dog, Fred, yelps a hello.
Howdy-do, Ruby and Eden. And who's this fine young fella?
  Mr. Fitzpatrick asks.
My cousin, Winter, clear from Sunflower, Mississippi.
Old Fitz extends his hand, and Winter shakes it.
Interesting name, Fitz comments.
Born the first day of winter is why, my cousin explains
  again.
Thank the Lord you weren't born the first day of autumn,
  Fitz teases,
Be hard for a young man to contend with in life.
Mama laughs; Winter smiles, and so do I.

He's the last, I say once we're in the house.
The last what? Winter asks.
The last white person on our block.

Mama adds, *And since his wife died, his daughter's been after him to move to Tucson, near her.*

When we first moved here, I tell Winter, *there were five white families.*

Mama pipes up again. *But one by one,* FOR SALE *signs went up, and off they flew.*

I picture white birds flying away and tell him, *It's called white flight . . .*

Soon as Negroes come, most white folks go.

Winter shakes his head. *Sorta like down home. Whites separating themselves from us.*

Y'all still got a little Jim Crow here too, huh?

Before I can say anything, Mama frowns and says,

OK, enough. Winter's here for a nice time. Let's not talk about all that.

Right then, to help her change the subject,

the telephone rings.

The Plan

I pick up. *Hello?*
It's my best friend, Winona. *Is he there?*
I know she means Winter.
Ever since she saw his photograph, she's been dying to
  meet him.
I say, *Yeah, he's here.*
Is he as cute as his picture?
Because he's my cousin, I hadn't thought of him like that,
but I peek at him and answer, *I s'poze.*
Winona giggles.

By the time I hang up, Mama's busy cooking,
Daddy's head is buried in his newspaper,
and Winter's in the garage, on the piano, plinking.
I hurry out there to join him.

Can you teach me? he asks.

I'm no teacher.

C'mon, cousin, please.

I sit beside him on the bench, show him finger exercises,
    and he catches on quick.

I'm sharp like that, he brags.

Lickety-split, the conversation changes direction,

winds up at tomorrow, and Winter spells out his plan.

The first thing we'll do is go to where he was living,
    show his picture around,

ask questions, like they do on TV on Dragnet.

You have a picture? Can I see?

He pulls out his wallet. *That's him, J.T., holding me.*
    I was just three.

What's J.T. stand for?

Nuthin', just J.T. You know how country folks can be.

I grin from ear to ear.

On the back of the photo is an address on East 113th Street,
    Watts, California.

Inside my head, I calculate.

That's near Central. The bus won't take too long.

I hand him the picture, and once he safely tucks it away,

I decide the time for Eden Louise Coal to blab has arrived.

My friend Winona, whose party we're going to, saw your picture

and thinks you're cute. She's thirteen, same as you.

Winter stops playing, grins, and asks,

This girl, Winona, does she turn heads?

Huh?

You know, get eye traffic from the fellas.

Boys notice her, if that's what you mean.

That's what I mean, cousin, exactly what I mean.

Then I'm sure you'll like her, I tell him.

He chuckles, then says, *Hey, I just thought of something—*

Winona and Winter both begin with "Win." Must be a sign!

Steps in Different Directions

Daddy pokes his head outside. *Eden and Winter, y'all hurry,*
Lyndon Johnson's 'bout to sign the Voting Act of 1965!
Together, in front of the television, we huddle.
The president puts pen to paper and signs.

This is monumental, Mama declares, *a step in the right*
   direction.
Daddy cheers and proclaims, *Thought our hope had died*
   with JFK,
but LBJ might just do us right.
Immediately, Winter disagrees. *Some folks in Mississippi*
might still be too scared to vote, like my mama. You know,
after the Freedom Summer murders and the bombings
   of that Freedom School
and then those houses in Indianola just this past May . . .
Daddy hangs his head. *We knew some of those folks who had*
   their homes bombed.

It's why we left. *Too many folks wanting to kill us when we try
to claim our rights.*

Winter says, *I've been begging Mama to leave, move here to
California, where it's nice.*

Daddy, as always in the mood for truth, tells him,
*It may look nice, son, but even here it doesn't take long to learn
we're not always welcome. There may not be signs posted, but
segregation's alive here too.*

Plenty of places we can't rent or buy.

The Fair Housing Act was supposed to change all that.

But, of course, it was repealed.

One step forward, another step back.

The Drive-In Movies

After dinner, Mama announces, *We're going to the drive-in*
    to see Cat Ballou.
Daddy, who adores Western movies, adds, *Fellas at work*
    claim it's funny too. Plus, I wanna see Nat King Cole.
Hard to believe he passed away.
Y'all shake a leg.
Never been to the drive-in movies, Winter reveals.
That's three in one day, I say.
He gives me a funny look. *Three what?*
Three things you did for the first time: the pogo stick,
    no back of the bus,
and now the drive-in movies.
Mama says, *I expect California will give Winter lots of firsts.*
He replies, *Miz Ruby, you're probably right.*

It's crowded, but Daddy finds a good spot.

Then it's popcorn, soda, fun, and laughter.

Daddy claims Nat doesn't look sick at all,

but right away, Mama contradicts him.

Latecomers forget to dim their lights,

and someone backs into a speaker post,

interrupting the movie.

Hoots, hands clapping, howls, and horn honks

sound off when the show is over.

And this song of the night—a nocturne—

    which I will later call

"Winter's First Time at the Drive-In Movies," concludes.

What does Winter think of it all?

He smiles and says, *Outta sight!*

The Search Begins

Saturday morning, August 7, 1965

I wake up to the sound of an airplane overhead,
then birds chirping, followed by quiet.
I decide on green pedal pushers and a blouse with
   white daisies.
When I knock on Winter's door, he's already dressed.
On the breakfast table we find some dollar bills,
ten quarters, and the front-door key along with a note
   from Mama,
reminding us to be home by five for the party at Winona's.

I'm bringing a notebook and a ballpoint pen, I tell Winter.
That way we'll be able to write down clues,
phone numbers, names of witnesses, like real detectives do.
Winter says, *Good idea, Eden, very good idea.*

We walk down our street, and except for the Espinozas,
our other next-door neighbors, the block is empty.

Mr. Espinoza is mowing his lawn, and the smell of freshly
  cut grass is in the air.

I sneeze.

His kids, Isabella and Tony, are roller-skating
  on the sidewalk,

and Mr. Espinoza, the way he always does, greets me
  with a smile.

Buenos días, Señorita Eden.

Buenos días, Mr. Espinoza.

It means "good morning," I explain to Winter.

I figured. . . . Say it again for me.

Buenos días.

Buenos días, he repeats. *I'm adding that to my list, number 124,
learn to speak Mexican.*

I correct him: *Spanish, not Mexican.*

OK, number 124, learn to speak Spanish.

The Loudmouth

We're passing by Century Foods, our neighborhood market,
on the corner of Century and Figueroa, when I hear her.
Hey! Eden! Eden! Eden!
Loudmouth Polly Parker. She's right behind me
but, as usual, hollering just the same.
Standing next to her is her identical twin sister, Penny,
who may look like Polly but isn't a loudmouth.

They live on 103rd Street, too, at the corner of
   Denver Avenue,
and for the past two years we've gone to the same school.
But because Polly is too rowdy and boy crazy for
   Mama's liking,
we are only sort-of-friends.

Who's this . . . your boyfriend? Polly yells.
No, he's my cousin, from Mississippi, visiting for two weeks.

Polly gets in Winter's face.

You are F-I-N-E! she spells out. *What's your name?*

Winter, Winter Robeson.

Penny smiles sweetly and softly says, *Winter. I love the snow.*

Of course, Polly pokes fun. *You haven't even ever been
     in the snow.*

Penny shyly replies, *But I've seen it on TV.*

Polly snaps back, *You are so ree-dic-u-lous.*

Am not.

I interrupt their back-and-forth by completing the
     introduction.

Winter, this is Polly and Penny Parker.

Polly steps away from her sister, singling herself out.

Don't get us mixed up! she advises him. *We may look alike,
     but we're not.*

*I'm Polly, and I'm the good dancer. I can do the Swim,
the Boomerang, and the Hitch Hike. Want me to teach you?*

Penny stares at Winter dreamily and tells him, *I can dance too.*

Polly sneers at her twin and clicks her tongue. *Don't listen to
     her, Winter.*

She doesn't even have a teaspoon of what I have.

What's that? he asks.

I got a whole lotta S-O-U-L!

Because I am used to Polly, I'm able to keep my cool, but
   Winter busts up laughing.
Luckily, the approaching bus saves us.
We have to go, I announce. *C'mon, Winter!*
But Polly keeps yakking. *Yesterday, we got four new records,*
including James Brown, the Miracles, and Wilson Pickett,
if you wanna come over!
Maybe, I tell her as we board the bus.

As we settle into our seats, Winter says, *The shy one seems nice,*
but that other one . . . does she always talk that loud?
Always, I reply.
He rubs his ears and declares, *She was about to bust both my*
   eardrums.

Betty West

At Central and Imperial, we step off the bus.

The first thing that happens is a man asks Winter,

Young brother, can you spare some change?

Winter reaches in his pocket and drops two quarters into
the man's hand.

Much obliged, says the man. *Much obliged.*

We pass a boarded-up motel and some run-down
apartments.

Winter takes it all in. *On the train ride here, I didn't
picture this.*

I ask, *What'd you think, California was gonna be perfect?*

Yeah, like the way it is on TV.

No place is perfect, Winter . . . well, except for Disneyland.

We walk a few more blocks and finally find ourselves
standing in front of the house

where Winter's daddy last resided.

Painted light green, it's surrounded by a chain-link fence.
In matching planter boxes near the front door are pretty
yellow daisies.
It's one of the nicest houses on the street.
Winter is about to open the gate when two German
shepherds barrel around
from the side of the house, barking and growling,
displaying sharp teeth, forcing us to back away.
From behind the screen door, a woman commands, *King
and Kong . . . get!*
And with that, the dogs retreat.

Winter opens his mouth, but before he can utter a word,
the woman starts up. *Whatever you're selling, I don't need it,
can't afford it, don't want it. Now, both of you, scat!*
Undaunted, Winter stands tall. *We're not selling anything,
ma'am.*
My name is Winter Robeson, and this is my cousin, Eden.
*I'm searching for my daddy, and this is the last place he lived
before he disappeared.*
I add, *Please, ma'am. He's come all the way from Mississippi.
We just want to ask some questions.*

The screen door swings open, and out she comes.

She's Negro, wearing a dotted blue dress.

Not that old but walking with a cane.

She studies us both, then aims her attention at Winter.

My name is Betty West. Now, tell me your story.

What little he knows about his father, Winter reveals.

As soon as he's done, Betty begins. *He's been missing almost*
  ten years, huh?

Well, our son bought this house for us about nine years ago, and
  I've lived here ever since.

On Winter's face, disappointment appears.

Any idea who he bought it from? I ask.

She replies, *Can't say I do. But from what I've been told, they*
  used to rent the rooms,

so lots of folks probably lived here. My son would know more,
  but he's out of town right now.

Flew to New York City yesterday.

She beams and proudly adds, *He's a very successful*
  businessman.

Winter requests, *Can you ask him?*

Be happy to. Soon as he gets back week after next.

Now Winter looks deflated. *Week after next?*

I tear out a page of the notebook, scribble on it, and hand it
    to the lady.
This is my name and phone number, Miz West.
Can you call when you find out? And, if it's OK,
    can we have yours?
She replies, *Certainly, but do you mind if we go inside? I'd like*
    to sit down.
Broke my ankle a while back, and it's still healing.
Are you all thirsty? she asks.

Inside, taking up half the living room, is a baby grand piano.
When Betty starts talking, I hear what she's saying, but *it*
    has my attention.
Most of the people who live on this block haven't been here as
    long as I have,
so it's likely they won't be much help to you either. Even so, I'll
    ask around.
The baby grand has gold lettering saying STEINWAY & SONS.
It's the color of ebony, polished and perfect.
I want to touch it but don't.

Betty West notices. *That was my husband's pride and joy.*
He passed on two years ago. My days are spent missing him.

She gets sad-eyed, and I pat her shoulder.

He played it like a virtuoso. I keep it to remind me.

Do you play?

Yes, ma'am, I do. Read music too.

I'm hoping she'll ask me to play, but suddenly she lights up and looks at Winter.

Just thought of something, she says, *that might be of interest.*

I open my notebook to write.

There was an old woman named Dorothy Loop who lived next door back then.

Spent her days in a rocking chair on the porch, collecting neighborhood chatter.

If there's anything worth knowing, she's the one to ask, if she can remember, that is.

Last I heard she has the Old Timer's. It steals some memories, you know.

Winter perks up. *You think she's home?*

No, no, moved over to the Westside to live with her daughter somewhere near Crenshaw and Washington not too long after we moved in.

I'll see if I can get you her daughter's name.

And like I promised, I'll ask around. What'd you say the daddy's name is?

I write it down for her.

Out loud, she reads, "*J. T. Robeson.*" *What's the J.T. for?*

Nuthin', just J.T., Winter answers.

Betty West smiles. *Country people, huh?*

Yes, ma'am.

We thank her and are about to head off

when Winter asks if he can take a picture of her house.

Of course you can, son.

Thank you, ma'am, Winter tells her, and he snaps a picture.

Betty West's last words are *You two come back and visit
    anytime.*

And I wish you the best of luck.

The Supposed-To Man

We travel east toward the Towers.
We got a good lead, Winter, don't you think?
He shrugs. *S'poze I thought it would be easy, some kind of*
miracle.
Plus, I want to prove her wrong.
Who? I ask.
My mama. She ain't had anything nice to say about him.
Why?
'Cuz he broke his promises. So . . . she calls him the
supposed-to man.
Supposed to send for us.
Supposed to give her a better life.
Supposed to love her and me
more than anyone else on earth.
Last letter she got claimed he'd gotten a good job on the docks,
things were looking up, and he'd send for us soon. Then,
nuthin'.

Winter Robeson gets that look,

one that confesses he really wants to cry but won't.

I can see he's boxing with his feelings,

fighting hard to keep the tears away.

He needs quiet now, I figure.

For a while, we stroll without talking.

Clear to the Moon

Winter inspects the Watts Towers,
running his hands along the colorful mosaics, and asks,
Why do you think this guy, Simon Rodia, built these?
But before I can answer, he says, *S'poze it's a silly question,*
    huh, like asking why
an artist paints a picture or a musician writes a song.
I reply, *Because they want to?*

We marvel at the patterns of colored glass, seashells,
mirror pieces, broken tiles, the way the metal
    twists and curves,
until Winter comes to his own conclusion.
Naw, it was in his soul, and he had to. Same as folks up and
    down the Delta,
playin' and singin' the blues.
I wonder right then if I have the blues inside my soul and ask,

Do you think you have to have the blues to write the blues?
He shrugs and says, *More than likely.*

Later, he cocks his head back, stares upward to the tip of
    the tallest tower, and chuckles.
Maybe he figured he'd make it clear to the moon
    if he kept going.
I nudge him with my elbow. *You gonna add building*
    something like this to your list of things to do?
Naw, he tells me. *Something this amazing would take decades*
and siphon off my ambition, making it hard for me to
    accomplish anything else on my list.
He puts a new roll of film in his camera, takes a lot of
    photos, and asks a man to take one of us,
standing side by side in front of the towers.
The man says, *Say cheese.*
Cheese.
Click.

Party Time

We leave for the party at Winona's house in our finest.

Mama's dress, a bright floral print, is cinched at the waist

with a patent leather belt.

Daddy's gray suit pants are fresh from the cleaners,

and he's wearing a bow tie.

Winter's black slacks are a little short at the ankles

but not so much that it'll cause anyone to poke fun.

My favorite outfit, a navy-blue sailor dress,

has a white collar and big red bow.

Where are you going all dressed up? Cassie's mother,

   Miz Webber, asks

as she waters their front lawn.

Party at the Youngs' new house, Mama replies.

They moved over to the Negro Beverly Hills, didn't they?

   Miz Webber says.

Mama answers, *Yes, to Baldwin Hills.*
We all tell her good night.
And as Daddy steers the car toward the Westside,
the first evening stars drop into the sky.

The streets leading up to Winona's curve this way and that.
Below us, the city of Los Angeles comes into view,
all aglow and postcard perfect.
Some of the houses are big and what Daddy calls modern,
which leads Winter to comment, *Your friend, the head turner,*
    must be rich.
Unfortunately, Mama hears him. *Head turner?*
He means Winona, I explain.
Because boys sometimes turn their heads to watch her when
    she walks by.
Mama raises an eyebrow. *Winona Young, already a head*
    turner. . . . Is that so?

Music from the house floats toward us.
Daddy rings the bell, and seconds later, the head turner
    opens the door.
Instantly, Winona zeroes in on Winter.

And for a moment, as they check each other out, I feel
  invisible.

Daddy clears his throat, startling Winona out of her daze.
Hi, Mr. and Miz Coal . . . Hi, Eden.
As if she doesn't know, I introduce her to my cousin.
Winter laughs nervously.
Winona twirls a lock of her hair and grins.
Can we come in, Winona? Mama finally asks.
The head turner apologizes and ushers us inside.

The house is alive with music, dancing, laughter, conversation.
Winona's parents make their way toward us.
Hugs and handshakes and howdy-dos follow.
He's even cuter than his picture, Winona whispers.
She's wearing lipstick, pointy shoes with heels,
and a minidress, and has earrings in her pierced ears.
I finger my earlobe.
Why won't Mama let me get mine pierced?
Suddenly, my sailor dress feels little-girlish.
But when Winona smiles, then starts grooving to the music,
my happiness blooms.

She takes Winter by one hand, me by the other,
and drags us to the living room.
Now a trio, we dance to Jr. Walker and the All Stars'
    "Shotgun."
From that moment on, the party is pure fun.

The Beans Get Spilled

Sunday, August 8, 1965

Finally a warm day, perfect for the beach.
After church, we make a quick trip home, gather everything,
and are almost out the door when the telephone rings.
Mama answers. *Yes, she's here. . . . Who's calling, please?*
Curiosity crinkles my mama's face. *Betty West?*

Winter stiffens with surprise.
I take the phone. He hovers nearby.
Miss Eden? Betty says.
Yes, ma'am.
I got you the answer to one of your questions.
Which one?
The name of Dorothy Loop's daughter.
Can you hold on, Miz West? I want to write it down.
I make a beeline to my room and return with my notebook.

Betty West starts talking. *Her name is Antoinette Williams,*
   but she calls herself Toni.
Husband is named John, John Williams. Couldn't get an exact
   address, just Washington near Crenshaw,
like I told you, but I'm working on it.
I'll call you if I find out anything else.
I thank her. *Bye, now.*

Of course, Mama inquires, *What was that about?*
My eyes settle on Winter. *Can I tell them?* I whisper.
He says yes, and I spill the beans, fast.
And once I finish, Daddy says, *So, you two are playing*
   detective?
Winter's eyes tear up. *Not playing, sir.*
He retrieves the photo of him with his father and shows
   my parents.
I just want to try and find out what happened to him,
he explains. *People can't just vanish, can they?*
Mama studies the picture. *We'll ask around too,* she promises.
Daddy squeezes Winter's shoulder and tries to comfort him.
   Now . . . now.
Like the moments right before sunrise, a stillness comes.

That is until, in the driveway next door,

Maurice, the noisemaker, shoos away the blues.

Boing! Boing! Boing!

Smiles appear, and laughter too.

A Meteor from Outer Space

We're loading the car when Daddy warns,
Y'all be careful with this detective business, you hear? Wouldn't
   want trouble to find you.
We're not looking for trouble, Daddy, I assure him.
Nossir, didn't come here looking for that, Winter confirms.
But Daddy cautions us again.
Sometimes, looking for it or not, trouble pinpoints your location
and, like a meteor from outer space, lands right on top of you.
I search the sky and tremble.

At the Beach

The windows are down, flooding the car with August warmth,
as we drive toward the beach at Playa del Rey.
Music from the radio plays, and Mama has her scarf tied
    under her chin and sunglasses on,
reminding me of a glamorous Hollywood star.
I know we're getting close when I get a whiff of the salty
    ocean smell
and noisy gulls appear, swooping.
The sky is a perfect blue.

We arrive after one P.M. but, lucky for us, are still able to
    find an unclaimed firepit.
And when Winter peels down to his swimming trunks and
    sprints toward the water,
like a shadow, I am right behind him.
Quickly, the sand toasts my feet, but instantly, the water
    cools them.

Beside my cousin, Winter, I stand, and together the horizon
   of the Pacific we scan.

The ocean's splendid, ain't it, Eden?

My smile is a yes.

In the distance, boats sail.

Ever been sailing? he asks.

No, not yet.

Something else to add to my list. Number 125, learn to sail a boat.

A question I've had for a while appears.

What's number 1 on your list, Winter?

To find my daddy, of course!

He's waist-deep when he waves me toward him.

C'mon, Eden!

I make sure my swimming cap is on tight and wade into
   the water.

And sometime later, Daddy appears at the shore.

Y'all come eat! he shouts.

We sip icy colas, chomp grilled hot dogs, devour an entire
   bag of potato chips
and gobs of roasted marshmallows, until, finally,
   our stomachs are full.

Winter glances at the other beachgoers and comments,

Got white folks at this beach too.

I nod yes.

Silently, he studies the scenery.

Then, like sea lions, we bask drowsily under the sun
and discuss the new piece that's been added to our puzzle.

Winter beams with happiness.

We're getting close. I just know it.

Mama glances up from her magazine, eyes full of doubt.

But his are fixed on the sky, so Winter doesn't see her
    disbelief,

and I am glad.

Narrowing the List

There's one thing on our minds when we get home.

I grab the phone book, and the hunt begins

for Dorothy Loop's daughter, Antoinette Williams.

Got jillions with the name Williams, Winter comments.

Because he made a rhyme, I giggle, then say,

There has to be a way to narrow the list.

My thinking cap now on, the solution pops up.

I get the telephone, dial the operator, and ask,

If you live near Crenshaw and Washington, what do the

    telephone numbers start with? . . . Seventy-three?

    Thank you.

We pore over row after row, marking each one,

but still, so many possibilities remain. I am thinking,

    Now what?

when Winter, who must be reading my mind, exclaims,

I know what we need, a map!

I shout, *Daddy has one!* and make a dash.

My father's head is buried in the newspaper when I ask,
Daddy, can we borrow your map book?
He peeks up. *It's in the trunk of the car.*
Armed with the map book, we zero in and
    start making calls.
Despite letting it ring many times, some don't answer.
They're put on the callback list.
Quite a few deny knowing anyone by those names.
Two hang up as soon as I start asking questions.
It's taken over an hour to shorten the list down to ten.
Our TV dinners are ready, and *Lassie* is on.
And so, for today, the search comes to an end.

Dorothy Loop

Monday morning, August 9, 1965

By the time I wake up, Mama and Daddy have already left
    for work.
Some spending money and another message accompany the
    door key:
Call me at work if there's an emergency.
Be safe and be home by 5:30. Mama

Right after breakfast, Winter and I make more calls and
    slash our list
from ten Williamses to four.
Winter studies the map and points out,
These last four are not that far from each other, Eden.

In no time at all, we're back on the bus, but this time
    instead of going east, we're heading west.

At Crenshaw Boulevard we go north.

Is this Washington? Winter asks each time we come to a stop.

Finally, he apologizes. *Sorry for being impatient,*
but I've been picturing this for a really long time,
and it happened much faster inside my mind.

I decide to switch subjects, hoping it'll calm him down.

Winona thinks you're even cuter than your picture.

Nervously, he picks his fingernails. *Yeah, she's real cute too.*

But I can tell by his faraway look that J. T. Robeson occupies
    his thoughts.

Nevertheless, I don't give up. *She really wanted us to*
    come over, so maybe tomorrow.

He scans the map book page.

It's still a ways, huh? I don't want to miss it.

I promise him, *We won't.*

Once more, I try, but this fish has no interest in my bait.

So I surrender, stare out the bus window,

change my own focus to life's ongoing orchestra,

and picture myself, a conductor's baton in hand,

directing today's performance.

First door we knock on, no one knows Dorothy Loop
or Antoinette Williams who calls herself Toni.
The next one is the same. At the third, no one answers.
Disappointment hits him hard.

Maybe the last house, I say in a cheerful way.
Winter only shrugs, and to Wellington Road we go.

The neighborhood is what Daddy calls ritzy,
but the word Mama would use is elegant.
I spot our last house, and it is big and beautiful with a very
    long porch.
But the very best thing about it is that sitting right there
on that porch is an old Negro woman rocking back and forth.
I point and shout, *Winter! Look!*
We sprint, and in seconds we're standing in front of her.
Dorothy Loop? I blurt.
Yes, but I'm called Dottie by most. Except for my husband,
may his soul rest in peace. He always called me Dot.
My Oliver, he was a kind soul.
To her wrinkled face a distant look comes,
like the one Daddy gets when he recalls being a boy
and his mind takes a dip into the lake of long ago.

Moments later, she returns to the here and now and asks,
How can I help you?

Her skin is bronze; wiry hair, white.
Despite the day's warmth, she's wearing a sweater,
and a crocheted shawl covers her shoulders.
Winter's words fly fast.
Pleased to meet you, Miz Loop.
My name is Winter Robeson, and this is my cousin, Eden.
We got your name from Miz Betty West over on 113th Street,
    where you used to live.
Is it OK to ask you some questions?
She nods, and Winter repeats his story.
I know it's been nearly ten years, but maybe if you see his
    picture, you'll remember something.
Winter opens his wallet, shakes his head in disgust, and
    begins quarrelling with himself.
How could I do this? I can't believe it. I was looking at it last
    night and musta left it on the table.
How could I be so stupid?

Dorothy interrupts, *113th Street . . . Is that where we are?*
I reply, *No, ma'am, this is Wellington Road.*

Hoping someone else is home, I ring the bell.

No use in that, Dorothy informs us. *They're gone.*

To work? I ask.

*Somewhere. They'll be back after sundown. Even Josiah goes out
     sometimes.*

Like a little kid, she giggles, then whispers, *I have a secret.*

What? Winter asks.

Y'all give your word not to tell anyone?

We promise.

Somehow, I caught amnesia.

Carefully, she readjusts her shawl, resumes rocking, and
     asks again,

How can I help you?

Winter doesn't know what to say.

She's like a musician

who has forgotten her notes,

it occurs to me.

The Police Station

We'll be back tomorrow, we tell her, and Dorothy smiles and
    waves goodbye.
As we stroll down Wellington Road, I'm doubting she'll
    even remember.
Baldwin Hills, where Winona lives, is nice, but this
    neighborhood is even prettier.
Mama would love it, I know. It would fit her
    top-of-the-mountain dreams.
For a moment, I picture her here.
I glance at Winter, who is silently fuming, angry at himself.
He's a dragon breathing fire. Words right now will make it
    worse.

After two blocks, his face goes soft, and I unbutton my lip.
*Strange for her to call it amnesia when it's Old Timer's, don't
    you think?*
Like a conquered foe, he replies,

Doesn't matter, Eden. Either way, the memories are still gone.

But where'd they go? They can't just vanish.

His stare stings, and I almost flinch.

Why not? People seem to is his answer.

I button my lip again but only for a while.

I've been thinking, I tell him.

About?

Going to the police station, asking some questions.

There's one on Broadway. A small detour on the way home.

Winter shakes his head in disgust and spews,

Mama and his folks back home already did that plenty of times.

And you know what the police finally told them?

What?

Some folks don't want to be found.

Hoping to persuade him, I say, *But maybe that's not true,*
    Winter.

Off into the distance he stares, then concedes. *OK, Eden.*

Luckily, there's no line at the information desk.

We're trying to find someone who's lost,

Winter says to the uniformed officer

whose badge reads CHARLES W. LAWRENCE.

A missing person?

Winter nods.

The officer shuffles around until he finds the form.

Missing individual's name?

J. T. Robeson.

Before Officer Lawrence can ask, Winter informs him,

The J.T. doesn't stand for anything, just J.T.

Male or female?

Male.

His date and place of birth?

April 22, 1928, Tupelo, Mississippi.

Officer Lawrence grins.

Same as Elvis Presley, he notes. *I'm a fan of his. S'poze most*
   folks never heard of Tupelo

until Elvis made it big.

S'poze not, sir.

You born there too?

Nossir, Sunflower.

Relationship to J. T. Robinson?

Not Robinson, sir, Robeson. Lots of people get that wrong.

Winter spells it out, *R-O-B-E-S-O-N.*

Your relationship to J. T. Robeson?

I'm his son.

Your name?

Winter Robeson.

Winter, like the season?

Yessir.

He writes that down.

How long has he been missing?

Almost ten years.

That's when the Elvis fan stops writing.

The look he gives Winter is long and dubious.

Loudly, he sighs, then asks,

And this is the first time anyone's reported him missing?

Nossir.

I cut in and explain, finally ending with,

And now my cousin is here visiting for the first time.

So I convinced him he oughta come to the station,

just in case you have some new clues.

Officer Charles Lawrence grins again.

And your name, miss?

Eden Louise Coal, sir.

His focus returns to Winter.

It's a long time for someone to be missing, son.

I know . . . but . . . shouldn't there be a file or something?

Should be.

The officer asks a bunch of other questions and
  jots it all down.

I'll have someone check and get back to you. It may take a while.

I'll be here until August nineteenth.

We'll try to have something for you by then, but can't promise.

By now, there's a line of people behind us.

The Elvis fan calls out, *Next!*

Learning the Boomerang

On the bus ride home, Winter sits with his
  shoulders hunched,
his face covered with defeat.
We'll find him, I promise.
Stoppit, Eden! Didn't you see the way that cop looked at me?
How?
He shoulda just come out and said it.
Said what?
I'm just wasting my time.
Sorry, Winter.
I'm ready to stop chasing this stupid dream.
It's not stupid.
Cut it out, Eden. I'm not in the mood.

103rd Street is alive when we turn the corner.
The Espinoza kids are playing hopscotch.

I'm winning, Eden, Isabella brags.

Maurice is on his pogo stick. *Look, Eden! One hand!*
 he boasts.

Cassie, singing along to the radio with her feet propped up,
 gives us a wave.

Coming toward us from the other direction are
 Polly and Penny,

their rhythm a perfect walking speed—andante.

My cousin covers his ears. His timing is perfect.

Where have you guys been? Polly screeches. *We came over
 twice, and I brought a bunch of records!*

Some of the latest hits!

Soon, we are face-to-face.

What's wrong, your ears cold or something? Polly asks Winter.

I suppose Winter is, like Daddy, a truth teller, because he
 says,

*Not trying to hurt your feelings, Polly, but has anyone ever told
 you that you talk way too loud?*

Penny snickers. *I told her.*

Polly's eyes jump from Penny to me, then Winter.

I'm expecting one of her speedy comebacks, but instead
 she's silent.

Polly pouts for a while before she smirks at my cousin and
    snidely says,
*Not trying to hurt your feelings, Winter, but has anyone ever
    told you that you have a ree-dic-u-lous name?*
I can see she's astonished by Winter's reaction, a very long
    howl of laughter.

My daddy is home, says company is OK, and in no time flat,
we've got the record player on.
Side by side, we all do the Jerk.
And when Winter puts on "Stop! In the Name of Love,"
Polly, Penny, and I do a near perfect impression of
the Supremes: Diana, Mary, and Flo.
Soon, like a magnet, the music attracts Cassie, followed by
    Maurice.
We sing along with the Temptations, and Polly teaches us
    the Boomerang.
Cassie riffles through their collection and exclaims, *You
    have "The Name Game"?*
Before Cassie can even get the record on, Polly grins at
    Winter and sings,
Winter, Winter bo binter,
and we all join in,

Ba-na-na fanna fo finter
Fee fi mo minter, Winter.
Winter's grinning, his eyes aglow.
The tempo is playful and merry—giocoso.
It's good to see my cousin happy, and so I'm actually glad
that Polly and Penny and Cassie and Maurice have come
and we are grooving to the music and having fun.

Another For Sale Sign

The sun is almost down when Miz Webber calls,
Cassie and Maurice, time for dinner!
Polly and Penny are next to go, but before they leave,
Polly turns and loudly announces, *We're moving!*
One glance from Winter is all it takes, and suddenly she
    remembers.
In a softer voice, she adds, *West of Crenshaw is where
    we're going.*
Mama says it's nicer, plus the schools are better there.
My face, I know, shows surprise.
First Winona, now the twins.
It's not just *white flight*, I begin to realize.
Birds of other shades are flying away as well,
to places far, others near.
Along with them, Winter and I walk
to their corner of West 103rd Street.
A FOR SALE sign is already up.

Pacific Ocean Park

Tuesday, August 10, 1965

Plans to return to Miz Loop's are foiled today.
I have chores, and unbeknownst to us, Mama's made
    other plans.
Today will be spent with Winona at P.O.P.,
    Pacific Ocean Park.
Her daddy, we are told, will drop us off.
But we have a lead we need to follow, clues to be pursued,
    I explain.
Tomorrow is my mother's answer. *It's just one more day.*
Winter's face spells *setback*, but my feelings are
    divided in half.
Part is excited to go to P.O.P., and part wants to continue
    the search for J.T.
If you want, I can help, Winter offers as I pin the clothes to
    the line.

Working together, we finish up in half the usual time.
I examine him for any trace of sadness but detect zero.
Some music has a flexible tempo—rubato—
and Winter, it seems, also goes with the flow.

Winona's daddy honks the horn many times,
    as he always does.
Into the back seat we slide, say thank you and our hellos.
Winona keeps turning around, gazing at Winter, trying to
    memorize him,
just like I did that first day when he arrived.

Today's song turns out to be all about sunshine and
    happiness.
Walking through the park, we laugh, jive, and joke.
We're a musical triad—composed of three harmonic notes.
And after the Sea Circus, off to the fun house we go.
Winter declares as we exit the Flight to Mars ride, *Just
    added something new to my list—
become an astronaut, number 126.*
Winona looks confused. *Number 126?*
He has a long list of things to do, I explain.

And as soon as we get off the submarine ride, going to the
    depths of the deepest blue ocean
becomes his number 127.

Are you serious about all that? Winona asks, impressed. *You're so
full of ambition!*

Winter pokes out his chest.

And I add, *More than anyone else I know.*

My list is a short one, Winona reveals. *To become a
    pediatrician.*

Now it's Winter's turn to fill up with admiration. *So the
    head turner . . .*

Oops, I meant YOU are smart too.

Winona laughs. *I know that's what you call me. Eden already
    snitched.*

He pauses before he says, *Winona, you and me, we must be
    destined for greatness—*

after all, our names both begin with "Win."

Feeling left out, I say, *Greatness doesn't depend on how a
    name begins.*

Winter nudges me playfully. *Of course it doesn't, cousin. I was
    just funnin'.*

A Second Search for Dorothy Loop

Wednesday, August 11, 1965

Because we stayed up past midnight playing Monopoly, we
    wake up late.
By the time we head back to Dorothy's, it's past noon.
Winter pats his back pocket, where he keeps his wallet,
    and chuckles.
This time I made sure I have the picture.
I stare up at him.
It's been less than a week since his arrival,
yet for some reason it feels as if he's always been here.
Next Thursday morning he'll be on the train again,
back to Sunflower.
I'm not sure how you can miss someone before they're gone,
but I sure seem to be.

We are making our way down Wellington Road when
  Winter announces,
I just added number 128 to my list. Can you guess what it is?
I shrug.
Number 128, own a house in a place like this one day.
I ask him, *Whatcha really want to be, Winter?*
Not exactly sure yet, just make my own path to greatness.
What about your list, Eden? What's on it?
I want to write music. I pause. *I think.*
You written any yet?
Some. They're not very good.
*Why you gonna talk yourself down? There'll be plenty of folks
  to do that for you.*
*You haveta believe in yourself, cousin. That's my rule number
  one.*
I ask, *What's your rule number two?*
Believe in yourself some more.
Thanks, I tell him. *I need to learn to do that.*
How, I wonder, if he's only thirteen, can he seem so much
  older?
Walking beside him, I feel young.

We reach our destination, expecting Dorothy Loop
to be on the porch, but she isn't.
And despite ringing the bell over and over
and knocking as hard as we can, there's no answer.
This we had not anticipated.
I'll leave a note.
No, he says. *Let's just wait,* then promptly plops onto Miz
    Loop's chair.
We can't. It's trespassing. We could get arrested.
Quickly, Winter jumps to his feet.
We decide to come back later.

Blocks away, we find a small park with kiddie toys.
For a while we play on the swings, seesaws, and monkey bars.
Then across the street we go to buy Cokes and chili dogs.
After a while, he insists we head back to Dorothy Loop's.
We do, but still no answer, and Winter's mood turns blue.
Again defeated, he sits on the steps and buries his face in
    his hands.
I glance at my watch. *It's getting late. I'll leave a note.*
And that's what I'm doing when from the house next door
comes a man who reminds me of Santa, pink cheeks
    and white beard.

Looking for the Williamses? he asks.

Miz Dorothy Loop, Winter replies.

Ambulance came and took her to the hospital this morning,
the man who looks like Santa informs us.

*Toni and John are probably still there, but unless he went
    with them,*

Josiah might be home. He lives in the guesthouse.

Check the gate. If it's locked, he's not here either.

Winter tries the gate. It's locked.

Which hospital, sir? I ask.

No telling. There are three close by. Are you family?

Winter tells a lie that's frosted with a truth.

Yes, I'm here visiting from Mississippi.

*Well, come on over. I'll let you use my phone to call the
    hospitals.*

We follow him, step inside one of the other pretty houses
    on Wellington Road,

and our second search for Dorothy Loop begins.

By the time we reach Cedars of Lebanon Hospital, it's
    almost five o'clock.

We're told which floor Dorothy Loop is on, and the elevator
    takes us up.

Are you family? the nurse at the station inquires.

For the second time today, Winter lies. *Yes, ma'am.*

She's in room 346. It's straight ahead down the hall.

Winter asks, *Will she be OK?*

We're always hopeful.

The polished floors of the hospital corridors gleam.

I take his shirtsleeve and guide him.

Only Dorothy and a huge vase of flowers are inside
    the room.

Like quiet breezes, we enter and huddle at her bedside.

She's sleeping, her chest rising and falling with each breath.

She looks very peaceful—*placido.*

Gently, Winter takes her hand. *Miz Loop, wake up,* he
    pleads. *I brought the picture.*

But her eyes remain closed.

Suddenly, behind us, a woman asks, *Who are you?*

Out of my skin, I almost jump. I turn toward her and
    stammer,

Um . . . we . . . Are you her daughter, Toni?

She's tall, Negro, pretty, wearing a gray dress.

Yes, and you two are . . . ?

Winter takes a deep breath and starts to explain.

Is This Just a Dream?

I'm Winter, and this is my cousin, Eden. We met Miz Loop the
    other day, and we thought
maybe if she saw the picture, she'd be able to help us.
Help you with what? Toni asks.
Find my daddy.
She has dementia, Toni explains. *Calls it her amnesia . . .*
so I doubt she'd be able to help you with much.
Winter keeps going. *I know, but she lived on the same street as*
    my daddy about ten years ago,
before he disappeared. I have his picture right here.
He pulls out his wallet to show her.
It's me with him, way back then. His name is J. T. Robeson.
Toni Williams squints, examines it closely, and gets a
    strange look.
I know this man. He lives in our guesthouse in exchange for
    helping out with Mama,
but his name's not J. T. Robeson, it's Josiah . . . Josiah Robinson.

Winter is all eyes and ears.

I am wondering if this is just a dream.

He's in the cafeteria with my husband, John, Toni tells us.

Let's go see.

Her high-heel shoes click, and her tempo's quite quick.

I'm fidgety; Winter is jittery. Toni presses the button.

It seems much too long before the doors finally open.

As the elevator descends, she becomes very serious—*serioso.*

If Josiah is your father, I suppose you should know.

What? my cousin asks.

He had amnesia for a while. It's where my mother got to calling
  it that from.

It's a joke between them. She sighs. *And he lost an arm in the*
  accident.

The word startles him. *Accident?*

Nearly ten years ago, hit by a truck on Central Avenue, he was
  crossing the street.

Just that day he'd gotten a job at the docks in San Pedro Bay.

Winter whispers, *Same as the letter said.*

By the time the doors open, Winter is speechless, his eyes
  wide with disbelief.

As we walk beside her, Toni keeps talking.

*Mama was in the crowd that watched the ambulance take him
away.*

*She'd seen him around, but he hadn't been there long, and she
never knew his name.*

*He'd been renting a room from the man next door, and he didn't
know much about Josiah either.*

*Just that he was from Mississippi and his last name was
Robinson.*

Winter interrupts. *Lots of people get that wrong, mistaking
Robeson for Robinson.*

Toni starts up again. *She had us find out what hospital he
was in.*

*Took some digging because his identification had been lost,
but we found him. And she made me take her there at least
twice a week to visit.*

*He's all alone, is what she would say. Mama is kind in
that way . . .*

Tears well up, but she keeps on.

*Josiah, once he was off the ventilator, went for rehabilitation to
learn to walk again . . .*

Oh, and he's blind in one eye.

Blind in one eye? Winter asks.

Toni nods and continues,

When he was discharged from the hospital, he moved into our
    guesthouse.

For a long time, he couldn't remember anything about his
    people, but once his memory started to return,

we asked if he wanted us to help him connect with them.

But he told us to leave it alone. It had been so long, and at that
    point he felt he would only bring them

misery. He claimed he was only half a man. And that they
    deserved better than half a man.

Winter bows his head. *This is blowin' my mind.*

But No Words Come

At last, we reach our destination.

My cousin, Winter Robeson, like a bull,

charges through the cafeteria doors, and I'm

   right behind him.

In seconds, we're in front of the only two Negro men

   in the room,

one with a black patch over his right eye.

Daddy?

Both men appear baffled, but the man with the patch

   more so.

It's me . . . Winter, Winter Robeson, your son.

The man with the patch opens his mouth.

He tries hard to say something,

but no sound comes out.

A Musical Concoction

What happens next is strange and curious,
sorrowful and joyous, bewildering and tender.

I'm an outsider peering in through a window,
   an eagle-eyed spy.
But I'm also onstage, a cast member in an opera.
The people in the cafeteria have become our audience.

To be perfectly honest, I didn't foresee this happy ending.
Mostly, like everyone said, I figured J. T. Robeson was dead.
But not wanting to burst Winter's bubble, I'd kept that to
   myself.

I hear them talking, observe the warm embrace of
   father and son.

J.T.'s wail makes me shudder. *I'm sorry, son . . . I'm so sorry . . . Forgive me!*

His sorrow is enormous.

But it's Winter's joy that makes me cry.
Though he's wiping away his own tears, his stance is triumphant.

From the corner of my eye, I catch Toni and John whispering.
They excuse themselves and head back
to Dorothy's bedside.

This is Cousin Eden, Winter tells his daddy.
I am eyed with confusion.
She's your cousin Ruby and her husband Ernie's girl, Winter explains.
Pleased to meet you, J.T., I say.
He studies me. *Likewise, little miss. Last time I saw you, you were about two.*
I came to California to visit them, Winter says.

But mostly, he came to find you, I reveal.
Ruby and Ernie living in California?
I nod. *Going on three years now.*

J. T. Robeson sighs and, as if weighed down by disgrace,
    hangs his head.
Moments pass before he asks, *How is your mama, Winter?*
    I hope she's OK.
Kinda, he replies. *She works real hard.*

My mama, Ruby, an arrow to a bullseye, penetrates my
    thoughts.
A glance at my watch reveals it's nearly seven o'clock.
She's worried, I know. Plus, a punishment's coming.
I say, *I'll be back.*

Remembering two phone booths at the entrance
    to the hospital,
I make a beeline. In goes the dime.
It doesn't even ring twice before she picks up.
Hi, Mama?
Eden Louise Coal, where are you?
At the hospital.

Ruby Coal screams.

The next thing I know, Daddy's on the phone.

What's happened? Are you hurt?

No . . . but . . .

He hurls another question before I can explain.

Is Winter hurt?

Nossir . . . but . . .

His interrogation continues, still no chance to squeeze in a
   word.

Then why are you at the hospital?

We found him, Daddy.

Found who?

J. T. Robeson.

I imagine his astonished look.

Another Reunion

J.T., Winter, and I head back to Dorothy's room.

Slowly, J.T. limps along.

I fill them in on my conversation with my parents. *Mama*
    and Daddy are on their way here.

They're excited to see you after all this time.

They can't believe it!

J.T. is silent—his face blank, neither happy nor sad.

He's mulling all this over, I figure.

I try very hard not to look at his shirtsleeve where there is
    no arm,

or the patch over his eye, the scar across his forehead, but
    I fail.

Winter, I notice, is examining him too.

John and Toni are outside Miz Loop's room when we arrive,

having a solemn conversation with a doctor.

Winter, J.T., and I stand back to give them their privacy.

My own mama died when I was four, J.T. confides.
Dottie's been like a mother to me. She's ninety-seven now,
has lived a good life.

When we're allowed into her room, J.T. kisses her forehead
and kindly says, *Dottie, it's me, Josiah.*
She opens her eyes and gives a weak smile.
This is my son, Winter, he tells her.
Nice to meet you, she whispers, then dozes again.

Visiting hours now over, the five of us gather outside
   the hospital.
J.T.'s arm is wrapped around Winter's shoulder.
Toni and John . . . I'm about to go visit with my people awhile,
   J.T. tells them.
Toni admires Winter and claims, *He's the image of you,*
   Josiah . . . I mean, J.T.
How'd you get that name, Josiah? Winter inquires.
Miz Dottie's idea. Insisted it wasn't right and proper for a man
   to go through life with just initials.
It's Hebrew . . . means "healed by Jehovah." Considering
   everything I'd been through,
she figured it was fitting.

I ask a question. *What about the Robinson?*

Mistake that was made. By the time I'd remembered my real
  last name,

I decided to just let it be. Staying lost was pretty easy after that.

I knew it wasn't really right, but . . . I kept telling myself it was.

The times I picked up the telephone and nearly called y'all

are almost too many to count.

Toni pats J.T. tenderly.

Trouble in Watts

If sympathy could be measured, the amount Mama and
   Daddy have for J. T. Robeson
would weigh a ton.
It's not in their words, just everything else.
We've been driving awhile when Mama says,
Winter finding you after all this time is a small miracle, J.T.
But it's Winter who replies, *Nuthin' small about it. It's colossal,*
   Miz Ruby.
J.T. responds, *Amen to that.* And moments pass before he adds,
Nice automobile y'all have.
Mama smiles. *California's been good to us.*
Daddy nods in agreement, but J.T. doesn't say a word,
and I wonder if he's thinking what I am—that if he'd never
   come to California,
the accident that changed his life forever wouldn't have
   happened.
There are so many feelings bouncing around inside the car,

it's almost impossible to catch them all—
Winter's happy contentment, Mama's lingering surprise,
J.T.'s love dusted with sorrow, Daddy's serious concern.
But I am mostly puzzled about what the future is
    going to deliver.
Will Winter's mama, Inez, forgive J.T., who she bitterly
    named *the supposed-to man?*
Will J.T. go back to Sunflower, or like Mama, has
    California,
even despite the tragedy, gotten inside him?
After ten years, I figure it has.
I am still sorting through all of that when suddenly
my thoughts turn to Dorothy, mostly called Dottie.
I'm glad she was able to wake up long enough to see that
the man she'd been like a mother to and had named Josiah
was now reunited with his own son, standing there right
    beside him.

We have just crossed the threshold into the house when
    Winter asks,
Cousin Ernie and Miz Ruby, can I please call my mama? It's
    long distance, but I have a little money.

Go ahead. And you can keep your money, Winter,
  Daddy tells him.
But just as Winter reaches for the phone, it rings and he
  picks up. *Hello?*
Yes, ma'am, she's here. Just a minute. Miz Ruby, it's for you.
  Miz Young, Winona's mama.
My mama takes the phone. *Hello, Marlene.*
I watch as she listens intently. There's no smile on her face.
I wonder if something bad has happened and hope Winona
  is OK.
She ends the call with *Thank you for calling, Marlene.*
Her worry face is now on.
Which leads Daddy to ask, *What was that about?*
Marlene just got a call from the NAACP. Something's
  happening over in Watts with the police,
and folks are carrying on.
What exactly? Daddy asks.
Mama answers, *Arrests were made, fights broke out, folks*
  rising up and shouting about
police brutality and all the rest. Quite a mob, Marlene says.
And that's when Daddy puts on what Mama calls his
  preaching voice.

Not surprised folks are riled up. Long history of police
  harassment and brutality there.
Negroes in Watts better not say boo unless they want to wind up
  roughed up or handcuffed.
Josiah agrees. *So true.*
Daddy keeps the ball rolling. *Its schools are mostly half rate;*
  grocery markets, lousy.
Plenty of folks don't have jobs, and some who do have to travel
  for hours to get to them
because they're shut out from renting and buying outside the
  Negro areas.
His sermon continues. *Most feel like they don't have a voice,*
  and when they talk, no one listens.
Daddy rubs his chin the way he does when he's thinking
  and asks, *Where exactly is the trouble?*
Near Imperial and Avalon, Mama tells us.
I say, *That's near Betty West's house.*
Where I used to live, J.T. adds.
Daddy rubs his chin again and promises,
It'll probably settle itself down by the morning.

Right or Wrong

My cousin, Winter Robeson, places the long-distance call,
and it's a while before anyone picks up.

Nana! Is Mama awake? Can you wake her up?

Seconds later, *Mama! Wake up good! I need you to wake up
real good because*

you're not gonna believe this! I found him, Mama . . .

J. T. Robeson, my daddy!

And he's not the supposed-to man, Mama . . . he's not!

Winter cries.

Before long, Winter motions J.T. to the phone, but Daddy
steers him toward their bedroom.

*I believe privacy's in order. Use the phone in our room. Talk as
long as you need.*

J.T. disappears into the room, and Daddy shuts the door
behind him.

It's a warm night, and Mama opens the front door.

Could use some air in here. Don't you think?

Through the screen comes a breeze and the faint sound of
mariachi music from the Espinoza house next door.
Far off in the darkness, sirens blare.

Later, J.T. and Winter decide that Winter will go
and stay the night at his father's place on Wellington Road.
Winter confides as he packs a few things,
I'm afraid if he's out of my sight something else
might happen, and I can't lose him again . . . I just can't,
as if keeping two eyes on a person
can somehow prevent misfortune.

I wait up with Mama while Daddy drives them home, and
    we talk.
He thinks he's only half a man, I tell her, *and Toni*
    claims that's why
he never got in touch with Winter and his mama when he got
    his memory back.
What do you think? I mean, if Daddy only had one arm
    and one eye,
I'd still want him near me, wouldn't you?
Mama replies, *Of course I would. Two arms and two eyes are*
    not what make a man a man.

But I hadn't finished with my questions. *Do you think he was*
   right or wrong?
Not having walked in his shoes, she answers, *it's not for me*
   to say.
Just glad Winter has him back, happy for Inez too. It was hard
   on her, not knowing,
thinking the worst. Nothing about the past can be changed,
   Eden Louise.
He's alive. I think he should walk forward without any shame.

That night, before I close my eyes,
I give up wondering about whether it was wrong or right
and decide to be happy—for Winter.

The Riots

Thursday, August 12, 1965

When I walk into the kitchen the next morning,
the headlines on Daddy's newspaper grab my attention.

1,000 RIOT IN L.A.
Police and Motorists Attacked

What Mama called carrying on last night is now being
    called a riot in the news.
One thousand people? How can they be so sure about that
    exact number? I wonder.
Did someone count them one by one, or is it just a guess,
like the number of gumballs in a machine?

For the first time in nearly a week, the house is empty
    except for me.

My morning song is a solo.

Next to the newspaper, Mama's note instructs me that
no matter what,

because of the trouble in Watts, I am not to leave the house.

And I'm to call her at work if there's an emergency.

I look outside.

Across the street, flocked together like birds, a cluster of
neighbors are gathered.

Miz Webber, Maurice, and Cassie are there; Polly and
Penny and Fitz too.

Miz Espinoza crosses to join them. Behind her, Tony and
Isabella scamper.

Quickly, I dress. I don't mean to disobey Mama,

but I need to step outside for a minute to see what's going on.

In unison, I am greeted. *Morning, Eden.*

There was rioting last night, Fitz reports.

Down there in Watts, Miz Webber adds, making it sound
like a faraway place.

She keeps talking. *Attacking the police, burning up cars.*

That's why we're moving, Polly proclaims. *This is much too
close to that Eastside mess.*

Maurice gets on his pogo stick. *Boing! Boing! Boing!*

His mother makes him stop.

Miz Espinoza advises, *We should all probably go inside.*

Cassie removes her radio's earphone. *This isn't Watts.*

It's not that far, I remind her.

She and her mother give me disapproving glances.

What if it spreads? Penny asks, making it sound like a
   contagious disease.

Maurice, carefree as usual, begins bouncing again.

Boing! Boing! Boing!

Tony and Isabella start playing tag,

their darting movements happy, playful—scherzo.

I am smiling, glad that here, just west of Figueroa,

it still sort of seems the same as most other summertime days.

I'm about to go inside when a police car, lights flashing,

rolls toward us and stops where we're standing.

The officer who's driving rolls down his window and asks,

What's going on?

Fitz answers for the group. *Not much, Officer. Just having a
   neighborly conversation.*

At that moment, the other policeman steps out of the car
   and commands,

OK . . . you folks need to disband! Now!

But we're not rioting, sir, I inform him.

Warning me to hush, Miz Espinoza nudges me and puts her
    finger to her lips.

Well, break it up right now! the officer orders.

Break what up? Maurice asks snidely.

Quickly, the policeman draws his gun and points it at
    Maurice.

Miz Webber yells, *No!* and instantly becomes
    her son's shield.

Cassie leaps toward her mother.

Fear freezes the rest of us.

That's when, luckily, the police radio sounds off and the
cop hurriedly climbs back into the car and speeds away.

A tear rolls down Miz Webber's cheek.

Maurice, wrapped in her arms, is quivering.

Fitz is shaking his head in disbelief.

Polly and Penny, holding hands, are as quiet as butterflies.

Miz Espinoza is holding her children close. I am trembling.

Cassie's transistor radio, dropped in the frenzy, is broken
    into pieces.

In Full Bloom

One by one, we, the residents of 103rd Street,
just west of Figueroa, not too far from Watts, rush back to
   our houses.
And fear, like one of Mama's prized roses, is in full bloom.
It's a perfect example of musical dissonance—tension, clash.

I part the front window curtains enough to see
   but not be seen.
My hands are still trembling.
Like a TV rerun, it replays inside my head.
I see the officer, the gun pointed, Maurice's terrified face,
until the fright, growing inside me,
gets too big to contain, and finally
my tears slowly trickle.

It's one of those I-wish-I-weren't-alone times, but I am.
I could call Mama, but that would lead her to ask why,

when she had instructed me not to leave the house,

was I outside in the first place?

And what on earth was I thinking, talking back to
     the police?

So, instead, I call Winona.

She asks, *Were you scared?*

With her, I don't need to pretend. *Yes. Really scared!*

Well, you and Winter should come over here.

He's gone.

Back to Mississippi?

No. Then I remember, I haven't even told her.

He found his daddy, I explain.

As I'm telling the story, I realize that he, my cousin,
     Winter Robeson,

can cross number 1 off his list!

Winona and I talk for a while the way we usually do, about
     some of this, a little of that.

But my mind is still occupied by what just happened, and I
     only half listen.

She got a new outfit, all black-and-white polka dots.

You can still come over by yourself, and we can go swimming,
     she insists.

I call to ask Mama, saying nothing about what has
 happened.
She surprises me by saying yes.
Before long, Mr. Young's outside. As always, he honks
 several times,
and I am whisked away to the Westside.

As we drive, the new music of Los Angeles makes me
 uneasy.
A car backfires, and I flinch. A siren wails, and I cringe.
So I tune it out and begin to hum a snail-like Mississippi
 melody.
And after a while, peace comes.
Folks are saying things in Watts are settling down today,
 Mr. Young comments.
I reply, *I sure hope so.*

To Save Betty West

Friday morning, August 13, 1965

The headlines are huge on the front page of the newspaper.

NEW RIOTING
Stores Looted, Cars Destroyed

They lead me to conclude that what Mr. Young said about
   things settling down was untrue.
Of course, Mama's note orders me to stay inside,
and after yesterday's incident with the police,
being disobedient again is the last thing on my mind.

Fortunately, Winter's back, so today I have company.
But not so fortunately, the doctors say Miz Loop's taken a
   turn for the worse.

J.T.'s gone to see her, to be close to the woman who's been
    a mother to him.
J.T. said, *No point in Winter sitting with me at the hospital,*
    watching me grieve.
To me, that makes sense.

Even so, Winter seems happier than ever, still celebrating
    his colossal miracle.
While he scarfs down a bowl of cornflakes, I tell him all
    about yesterday.
I thought things like that only happened down South, he
    comments.
The phone rings, and Winter grins. *Maybe it's the head turner.*
But it isn't.
Miz Eden! This is Betty West. Can your people come get me?
Huh?
It's terrible! They set my car on fire! Plus, my dogs ran off with
    all the noise!
My son's still out of town, and I don't have anyone else.
She's been crying, I can tell.
I can't walk too far. Please have your people come and get me!
    she pleads.
I'll call my daddy, I tell her.

I call Daddy at the Department of Water and Power, but
    he's out in the field, they say.

Mama is next.

Tell her to call the police, she suggests.

*My daddy, who has the car, is away from the building, and
    Mama says you should call the police.*

I called them five times already.

And?

*If the police had come to help me, why would I be calling you,
    Miz Eden?*

Suddenly, there's the sound of breaking glass.

Betty West screams.

Miz West! I holler, and then the phone line goes dead.

Whatsamatter with Miz West? Winter asks.

*I dunno. . . . There was a loud crash, she screamed, then the
    phone died.*

Each time I call back, I get a busy signal.

I don't know what to do—but I can't just sit by and
    do nothing to help her.

Part of me is scared, but the part that isn't wins.

We gotta go! I announce.

Where?

To save Betty West.

The Air Tastes like Smoke

We figure my bicycle is the only way to go.
If Winter pedals and I sit on the handlebars, we'll get there
   fast.
Outside, Cassie is perched on their porch.
After yesterday, I'm surprised to see her there.
Where you two going? the gum smacker asks.
We ignore her and vamoose.

At first, it's calm, but the closer we get to Watts,
the more we see, smell, and hear.
And soon, we come face-to-face with war.
Billows of smoke rising, the stink of cars and other things
   burning,
sirens wailing, dogs howling, police and fire trucks ripping by.
Then heat from raging fires, gray ash, burning embers
   floating.
It's getting hard to breathe, and the air tastes like smoke.

Folks are running; mobs of people dashing, sprinting,
carrying anything and everything from stores.
A smiling woman tosses a pack of T-shirts at us.
We let it fall to the ground.
A man with a brick hurls it at a store window,
and shards of glass fly, just missing us.
I remember Daddy's warning about a meteor landing on me
and look to the sky.
The song of Watts is now warlike—bellicoso.
We shouldn't be here, but here we are.

Rescuing Betty

Betty's front window is broken, and the door is cracked.

Winter knocks, causing it to creak open.

Miz West! I call out. *It's Eden. . . . You here?*

Cautiously, we enter.

The rock that went through her window

is on the floor, surrounded by broken glass.

There's also a trail of blood.

Miz West! Winter yells.

No reply.

We follow the drops of blood until we finally find her

hiding in a closet, on the floor, scared to death and quivering.

A gash on her arm is bleeding.

She peers up at us strangely.

Miz West . . . it's us . . . Eden and Winter.

Oh . . . can't see you without my glasses. They fell off
  somewhere.

Winter finds them.

Y'all came for me. Didn't think you would.
Thank you. Is your daddy outside in the car?
she asks as we help her to her feet.
No, ma'am. We came on a bicycle.
It doesn't seem like a time to be laughing,
but she does, and so do we.

Winter examines her bleeding gash,
and I am wondering how it happened when she fills us in.
I slipped and fell on a piece of glass after that rock came through
  the window.
Why would someone do a thing like that to me?
You have a first aid kit, Miz West? he inquires.
Not sure you'd call it a kit, but there's some Band-Aids and
  other things in the bathroom.
He's back in a hurry.
Pressure should stop the bleeding, he advises, and shows her
  what to do.
Betty grumbles. *Folks in Watts are rebelling, aren't they?*
Newspaper calls it rioting, I say.
Winter says, *Never been in a war, but I s'poze it's kinda like this.*
My eyes land on the telephone. *Can I call my daddy,*
  Miz West?

Can't get a dial tone . . . not since I talked to you.

I pick up the phone and listen. Nothing.

It's all up to us now, so we talk and make a plan.

Soon, a wheelchair that was her husband's has been

retrieved,

an overnight suitcase has been packed,

and Winter has patched her window

with cardboard and tape.

Before we leave, I glance at the baby grand piano. It's still

perfect, and I'm glad.

Cover it up with a sheet, would you please? Miz West says. *It*

was his pride and joy.

Carefully, we drape it, then cautiously leave.

Mysterious Ways

Outside, a haze of smoke is everywhere.
As Winter pushes Miz West along the sidewalk,
I guide my bicycle alongside them, toward home.
Sure didn't expect this kind of thing in Los Angeles.
Sure didn't expect anything like this, she repeats.
I say, *Me neither.*
Then again, Betty goes on, *it isn't the paradise some of us*
　　hoped it would be.
Winter pipes up. *When I first got here, I was thinking it was,*
　　but now—
The sound of gunshots interrupts him, and a police car
　　whizzes by,
its tires shrieking as it swerves around the corner.
Winter picks up the pace, and Betty West clutches
　　her suitcase.

This time, hoping to avoid danger, we take the side streets.

But even closer to home there is trouble brewing, and

I know that what Penny feared is true.

This rebellion, riot, kind-of-like-a-war is spreading fast.

Blocks from home, it settles down some,

and all of the stuff we just saw and heard must have gotten
    shoved

into the back of Winter's mind, because he finally
    remembers.

So much happened just now that I forgot to tell you, Miz West!

His voice sounds like Polly Parker's—ear piercing—and it
    startles me.

Like a lit candle, his face glows. *Thanks to you telling us
    about Dorothy Loop,*

I found my daddy!

Betty West's stunned look is scattered with doubt.

She turns to search his face.

It's true, I assure her.

Where'd he been hiding for nearly ten years? she asks.

So Winter spills out his tale, and when he finishes,

Betty reaches back for his hand and squeezes it tightly
for a very long time.

*So Miz Loop, Old Timer's and all, led you to him. God works in
mysterious ways,* she preaches.

He certainly does.

Sorry, Daddy

Daddy's car is in the driveway.

Much too early for him to be home, I know.

He swings open the door and steps outside.

His arms are folded across his chest, and the closer I get, I see something

I've only seen in him a few times: anger, blazing like a wildfire.

Ooh, you're in big trouble, Eden! Maurice yells from his bedroom window.

Cassie told on you!

It's time to try a changing-the-subject tactic.

We saved her, Daddy! I proclaim. *Meet Miz Betty West!*

Betty grins and waves from the wheelchair,

and I note Daddy eyeing her bandaged arm.

Winter, trying to douse the anger, offers a defense.

Don't be too mad at us, Cousin Ernie. Wasn't for Miz West . . .

   I never would have found my daddy.

Then Betty, attempting to completely stamp out the flames,
  adds,
What fine human beings these two are.
There is a long pause—lunga pausa—
before Daddy's anger appears mostly extinguished.
And I say, *Sorry, Daddy.*
He takes a deep breath in and then out
as if trying to completely exhale his displeasure.
Until gradually, his face gets softer.

Some things are inevitable, and I know that I will be
  chastised later on—
it is one of those unable-to-be-avoided things.
Daddy forces a smile and greets Betty with a handshake.
Should have known Eden would have a handsome daddy,
  she remarks.
Daddy flashes a sheepish grin.
Betty winks at me, and I know that she's flattering him to
  lessen my penalty.

Finally, he turns my way. *Eden, put that bicycle in the garage.*
OK, Daddy.
Silently, I steer it toward the back gate.

You'll get it later, Eden! the noisemaker taunts.
If Maurice hadn't had a gun pointed at him yesterday,
I would have said something to really shut him up.
Instead, I just pretend he's not there.

When I come inside, I find Betty's face buried in a vaseful
  of yellow roses.
She inhales deeply. *Now, that's the sweetest thing I've smelled
  all day.*

Into the kitchen Daddy sends me to make sandwiches
  and lemonade.
He's turning up the television when I peer in.
The three of them have their eyes glued to the news.
The rebellion now has an official name.
The Watts Riots.

The National Guard Arrives

Saturday, August 14, 1965

Today, according to our itinerary, Mama and Daddy and
    Winter and I
are supposed to be at Disneyland, the Happiest Place on
    Earth.
But Watts is burning, people have died,
many more are injured, and the air still tastes like smoke.
A forty-six-square-mile curfew zone, which surrounds
all of the areas of Los Angeles where the majority of
    Negro people live,
is being enforced, making it a crime to be on the streets
    after eight P.M.
Of course, 103rd Street, just west of Figueroa, is included.
Roadblocks are being set up.
The National Guard has arrived.

And Fitz Is Gone

In the kitchen, Mama's making breakfast,
and the aroma of percolating coffee is everywhere.
Yesterday, Winter went back to be with his daddy,
and Betty West stayed in his room.
Daddy, sitting in his chair, glances up at me from the
    newspaper.
Our eyes meet.
So far, what my penalty will be remains unspoken.
I almost want to get it over with, or is waiting
a punishment of its own?

All of a sudden, there's a knock on the door that startles
    even Daddy.
Cautiously, he cracks it open.
Fitz?
Came to say goodbye, Ernie.
Mama flies in from the kitchen, and we crowd the door.

My daughter's hauling me off to Tucson, he announces.

Daddy invites him in.

Are you ever coming back? I ask.

Not if my daughter has her way, Eden, and knowing her . . .

His voice trails off.

He drops a set of keys into Daddy's hand. *I'm selling the house.*

If you'd be so kind to keep an eye on it for the time being.

Be glad to, Fitz. Is there a number where we can reach you, in case?

He rattles it off.

When Mama hugs Fitz, there are some tears in his eyes,

and while his dog, Fred, howls a very long goodbye,

he and my daddy shake hands.

I say to Fitz, *I sure wish you weren't leaving.*

Across the street, someone in a waiting car honks.

He says, *Bye, now,* and with Fred prancing beside him, he

saunters off.

Twice, he turns back to wave.

The car zooms away, and Fitz is gone.

I feel sorrowful—doloroso—and head to my room and shut

the door.

Right now, Eden Louise Coal needs to be alone.

A lot is happening; almost too much.

The tempo's been too fast. I almost want to scream.
Instead, I open my notebook and write about Fitz's departure,
this summer's latest chapter.

After a while Mama calls out, *Breakfast!*
The City of the Angels, a place, only days ago,
many called paradise, is going haywire.
Watts is like a war zone: troops are patrolling the streets;
citizens are being shot and killed; Fitz and others are fleeing.
Yet Mama has prepared the biggest breakfast ever.
Is she losing her marbles?
Or is she afraid this might be, like the Last Supper,
    our final meal.

And as if Betty is believing just that, before we eat,
she rambles one of the longest prayers that I've ever heard.
Each time I hope she's done, she isn't.
Daddy's head is bowed, but I can see his smile.
Finally, the amen comes.

Eden, Daddy says between mouthfuls,
Winona's parents have invited you to stay with them for as long
    as need be.

It's safer there—out of the curfew zone, away from all this.

I say, *But I wanna stay here with you and Mama and Betty.*

And it's not like

they're going to drop a nuclear bomb or anything . . .

are they?

Mama cuts in. *Ernie, I know the Youngs mean well, but Eden's*
   not going anywhere.

I need my only child where I can see her.

They catch each other's eyes, and I can tell that Mama is
   the victor.

There is silence until Betty says, *Please pass me some more of*
   those wonderful biscuits.

Growing Up

It's been less than a day, but Mama and Betty are clearly at
  ease together.
After breakfast, they're sitting at the kitchen table, sipping
  coffee and chatting,
and despite everything that's happening, now and then
  laughing.
I am busy cleaning up the kitchen.
Been here since the 1940s, Betty is saying.
*There weren't many Negroes here back then, but as soon as we
  went to war,*
*they needed us here for jobs at defense plants, and that was
  the lure.*
It's why Mr. West insisted we leave Little Rock.
Made a joke of it, saying the Wests are heading west.
*So many of us landed in Watts, not necessarily because that's
  where we wanted to be,*
but because it's where we were allowed to live.

Mama says, *Tried their best to steer us there, too, but I fell in love with this house.*

Outside, a siren blares, and Betty says, *It's just a shame. This is not a perfect city, no city is,*

but I never thought it would come to this.

Roadblocks and barricades penning us in like we're common criminals,

making it sound nice by calling it a curfew zone. Oughta just call it what it is . . .

the Negro zone.

I say, *Yes, and we're not all rioting or looting, but it seems like they're trying to make it look like we are.*

Mama's not smiling when she catches my eyes and tells me, *These are not things that children should be concerned with, Eden.*

Quickly, I reply, *But with everything happening, how can I not be?*

Plus, I've seen kids marching—remember the crusade in Birmingham? I remind her.

Some were even younger than me.

Mama clears her throat, my signal to be quiet, but I keep on.

This riot is happening to us, too, not just grown-ups.

Mama shakes her head. *Children's lives are meant to be carefree.*

I say, *Except, like now, sometimes they're not!*

This is when Betty interrupts us. She pats Mama's hand and
    says, *I don't know you that well, Ruby,*

but my tendency, like Eden's, is to speak my mind. May I?

Mama nods.

Did I mention that your home is very pleasing to the eye, Ruby?

Yes, thank you, Betty.

I am wondering, what has that got to do with all this?

Miz West continues, *And wouldn't it be wonderful if
    everything about life*

was as pretty as your lovely home?

There is a pause as Mama mulls this over before she replies,
    But it isn't, is it?

Betty pats her hand again. *We do our best to protect our
    children from the ugly chapters of life.*

*But there they are, right beside us through it all. We can't expect
    for them*

to pretend to be oblivious, can we, Ruby?

*No, Betty, we can't. It's just I want her to have a lovely life . . .
    not be worried all the time like I was as a girl.*

I can see the tears in Mama's eyes. *Children shouldn't have to
    be marching and all that.*

But, I say, *I really want to someday. Maybe even alongside
    Dr. King.*

These young folks are capable of bravery and good deeds,
   Betty tells her,
and I for one can't say where I'd be if Eden and Winter hadn't
   come to help me.
Mama sighs and meets my eyes. *You're growing up, I see.*
I smile. *Yes, ma'am, I am. It's something that happens to*
   everybody!

Even on Sunday

Sunday, August 15, 1965

The headlines are getting worse.

NEGRO RIOTS RAGE ON;
DEATH TOLL 25

And the riots continue, even on Sunday.

Outside, on 103rd Street, just west of Figueroa,
there is no *Boing! Boing! Boing!* from Maurice, the
   noisemaker;
no singing off-key from Cassie, the gum smacker;
no Isabella and Tony playing hopscotch or skating.
Our block is deserted—a ghost town.

There will be no church for us today.

From the window, we watch

as the National Guard patrols our block.

But unlike what I'd seen on the news,

their weapons aren't drawn.

So Many Goodbyes

Last night, Winter called and delivered the news.
Dorothy Loop, mostly called Dottie, passed away.
Her funeral is set for Wednesday.
I picture her kind bronze face, and tears fill my eyes.

Tomorrow, Betty's son will be back, and she'll go to his
    house to stay with him.
In just days, she and Mama have become fast friends.
And I like how Betty, same as lightning bugs, adds sparkle.
With Betty around, Mama plays her records a little louder,
and together they sing along with Ray Charles and
    Dinah Washington.
Betty smiles a lot, and Mama seems like her old
    Mississippi self.

First Fitz leaving, tomorrow Betty, soon Polly and Penny,
    next Winter.

I am feeling like the loser in a game of checkers,

my pieces being taken one by one.

I sprawl on my bed and write some more.

I've been keeping track of events every day as they occur,

and more than half of one of my notebooks

is filled since Winter Robeson came.

Sprouting Again

After I finish writing in my notebook, I head to the garage,
sit down at the piano, and play a song I wrote when we
first moved here and I was feeling homesick.
It's called "Longing for Indianola."
When I finish, Betty, behind me, claps.
I had no idea she was there.
Bravo, she says. *Who composed that?*
I reply, *Me.*
Oh my! That's a marvelous talent for a young lady to have.
Thanks, Miz West. My teacher in Mississippi, Miss Porter,
was teaching me most everything she knew, but then
     we moved here.
Do you still take lessons?
Yes, but my new teacher's nothing like Miss Porter—
when I told him I want to write music,
he reminded me that I'm a girl.

Miz West shakes her head. *Man must not know about*
  Julia Perry, she says.
I light up inside and say, *Yes! Miss Porter talked about her.*
What else have you written? I want to hear them all.
Only four more.
She plops in a chair. *Let's hear them, Miss Eden.*
I grab my composition book and begin to play.
She claps so loudly and continuously that you would have
  thought there
was a whole audience in that garage.
You remind of my mister. He had that kind of skill,
God rest his soul.
You share his gift, Miss Eden Coal.
And I applaud you.

Inside me, I sense what Miss Porter planted
sprouting again.
I picture the seed flourishing, growing into a tree.
Blossoming.

Feeling Gray

Monday, August 16, 1965

It's getting close to the eight o'clock curfew by the time
   Betty West's son,
Harold, shows up.
She's going with him to his house near La Brea and Pico.
We are thanked repeatedly and promised blessings for
   our help.
She'll come visit now and then, Betty assures us,
   if I promise to play piano.
And when Mama gives her a bouquet of roses, her delight is
   obvious.
Betty West has a gigantic spark of life, and when she departs,
it goes with her, leaving our house feeling as gray as the
   smoky skies outside.

The Riots Are Over

Tuesday, August 17, 1965

Finally, after six days, the Watts Riots,
rebellion, kind-of-like-a-war is over.
In all, thirty-four people died.
Twenty-three of them killed by police and the National
    Guard.
More than a thousand citizens of the City of Angels
have been injured, and thousands more arrested.
The air still tastes like smoke.

And *he* has come, the man Mama calls our saintly savior:
Dr. Martin Luther King, Jr.
He's saying violence isn't the way.
Some people agree.

Others don't want to hear it, because promises are always being made, but change is slow to come.
I'm hoping he'll lead a march
and I can be there with him.

Something Ordinary

I'm home alone, another solo performance,
when a knock on the door brings an unexpected surprise.
I fill up with happiness seeing Winter and J.T. come to visit.
Before I can ask, J.T. says, *Toni's husband, John,*
    dropped us off.
It's lunchtime, and I make tuna fish sandwiches
with sliced avocados and tomatoes the way I've seen
    Mama do.
Between bites, we talk.
Daddy's going back to Sunflower with me on Thursday.
That's in two days. My eyes tear up.
It's selfish, I know, but I want Winter to stay.
But if he's going, at least it's with his daddy, J.T.
I ask J.T., *You think you'll ever come back to California?*
To live?
Yeah . . . to live.

Can't say. Have to see how Mississippi feels and figure things
   out with Inez.
But if you don't come back to live, will you at least come back
   to visit?
J.T.'s grin is an exact replica of Winter's. *That's a definite yes,*
   Miss Eden.
Winter says, *Let's put it this way. You haven't seen the last of*
   us Robesons. That's for sure.
Plus, we never did get to Disneyland, and that's on my list.
I chuckle. *You and your list. I'm happy number 1 can be crossed*
   off of it.
Later, when we're alone, Winter says, *Think I should call*
   Winona before I leave?
I was thinking, you never know . . . I might need a good doctor
   one day.
When I scribble down the number, I smile, mostly
because it feels like this is such an ordinary thing
after many days of everything but ordinary.

Will It Happen Again?

Wednesday, August 18, 1965

The riots may be over, but Los Angeles is torn up in places.
You think it might happen again? I ask my mother.
Mama says she hopes not—that the politicians and church
    pastors
are saying things in Watts are going to change.
Promises are being made *again*, better schools,
    better housing,
more jobs and opportunities.
I hope they're telling the truth.
Dr. Martin Luther King, Jr., is still here.
But sadly, there won't be a march.
I want to see him anyway, to tell him that I plan to walk
    beside him someday.

Cautiously, for the first time in days, I venture outside.

From the sidewalk, I look up and down as far as I can see,

and hope 103rd Street, just west of Figueroa,

will soon be back to normal.

Whether Watts will ever be, I can only wonder.

Into the Sun

Thursday, August 19, 1965

Like it or not, the day of Winter's departure has arrived.
I am back downtown at Union Station—this time with
   Daddy and Mama,
the Williamses, Winter, and J.T.
Little did I know, fourteen days ago
   when Winter Robeson came,
just how unusual and unforgettable these two weeks
   would be.

Just like before, trains unload, and passengers stream out.
Hands begin waving, and people hurry toward each other,
smiling, reaching out arms, hugging, sometimes kissing.
But now, instead of hello, I am saying goodbye.
Please don't go, I want to beg.

We need more time to learn dances from loudmouth Polly,
visit the Happiest Place on Earth,
    wade in the Pacific Ocean,
then bask under the sun like sea lions.
And I want to teach Winter piano, hear him learn to speak
    Spanish.
I want him to share with me every single new addition to
    his growing list—
and everything that gets crossed off too.
I feel tears coming. And I don't even mind letting Winter see.

Winter puts his arm around me and asks, *Whatcha thinking*
    about, cousin?
I answer, *So many things.*
Well, just make sure whatever they are, you write them down
so you won't ever forget. So you can tell me when I see you again.
OK, promise?
I swear.
And keep writing music, promise that too?
That one's easy. *I promise.*

We all hug, wish each other well,
and then it's time to say our goodbyes.

At last, Winter and J.T. head off to board their train.

Winter's straw cowboy hat still looks too small for his head,

and for the second time, that makes me smile.

He and J.T. turn back and wave once, and I'm happy they
  have each other.

And then my cousin, Winter Robeson, is gone,

but not really, because he'll always be with me,
  inside my mind

in the place that stores our forever memories.

That will have to be enough for now.

I trail the Williamses, Mama, and Daddy

outside, into the sun.

An Extraordinary Day

Saturday, August 28, 1965

There has been a gradual slowing down of my life's
    tempo—rallentando.
And I am glad.
I'm washing the breakfast dishes. The kitchen window
    is open;
a warm breeze blows; the sky is blue again.
Some things have changed on 103rd Street, just west of
    Figueroa,
not too far from Watts.
Cassie doesn't have a new radio yet, so there's been no
    singing way off-key.
Polly and Penny have been sent to live with relatives on the
    Westside until they move.
So, for now, there are no more record parties inside my
    garage.

The Espinoza kids, Tony and Isabella, mostly play in their
   backyard.
But one thing has stayed the same, Maurice on his beloved
   pogo stick:
Boing! Boing! Boing!

And now all Mama talks about is moving, moving, moving,
following the others farther west, out of the curfew zone.
But Daddy is resisting, saying houses there cost too much.
Who'll be the victor, I can't foresee.
I dry the dishes and put them away.

After breakfast, Daddy buries his face in the newspaper,
   as usual.
Mama goes out to the backyard to tend her garden.
I head out to the garage and sit at the piano
to practice a song Miss Elvira Porter taught me.
Remembering her always makes me smile.

And that's where I am when Daddy comes and announces,
   Eden, you have a delivery.
Mama hears, and together, we hurry to the door.
A man is standing there. He asks Daddy to sign a form.

Outside is a large truck.

The man hands Daddy a letter. *It's for you, Eden.*

I open it and read.

> *Dear Eden,*
>
> *It is my pleasure and honor to entrust my dear husband's beloved piano to you.*
>
> *I know you will play it well and share your musical gift with the world someday.*
>
> *We are selling my house, and I am living with my son. I wanted it to have a good home and couldn't think of a better one than yours. You are in my thoughts and in my prayers. I wish you well and hope to see you soon.*
>
> *Sincerely,*
> *Elizabeth (Betty) West*

She gave me the baby grand . . . I have a baby grand piano!

I scream.

Where do you want it, ma'am? the man asks Ruby Coal.

In the living room, of course, Mama replies. *Where else should a baby grand piano be?*

It takes a while, but they get it inside.

And there it is. I don't need to wake up, because it's not a
    dream.
I trace the Steinway & Sons gold lettering.
Ruby Coal polishes it until it's perfect.
Daddy won't stop grinning.
Mama puts her arm around my shoulder. I feel so much
    love—amore.
I run my fingers across the keys.

And what began as an ordinary summertime day
takes an unexpected turn and becomes extraordinary.

The Concerto

I'm at my new piano, practicing advanced finger exercises,
when the mailman drops the mail through the slot.
As I gather it, I notice a letter addressed to me
from Winter Robeson, Sunflower, Mississippi.
I talked to him, a little, when his mama, Inez,
called us long distance just this past Sunday.
Hearing his voice had filled me with joy,
and when I told him about Miz West and the baby grand,
he let out a howl of extreme happiness.
I tear open the envelope.
Inside is the photo of us at the Watts Towers
along with a letter.

> Dear Eden,
>
> Everything in Sunflower is going fine. We're slowly
> getting used to being a family again, and that feels

nice. I'm sending you a copy of this picture of us at the Towers so you won't forget me, though I doubt that's possible because I am unforgettable like that. But just in case, I thought you might like it. Thanks again for helping me to find my daddy. Hopefully, the next time I come to California we'll have more time to sightsee (since we won't be snooping around or saving Betty West!). One more thing, cousin: remember I'm counting on you to keep writing your songs.

Until we meet again,
Winter

P.S. Say hello to the head turner for me.

The picture makes me smile, and I'm reminiscing when it
  dawns on me
to compose some music about those days with Winter.
It'll be a piano concerto, I decide, with changes in tempo
  from slow—largo—to fast—allegro.
A mixture of happy, sad, and strange—
  festoso, mesto, and misterioso—
the same way life, as I am learning, tends to be.

Of course, exactly like August of 1965, it will have an unexpected ending.

I sit down at the baby grand, open my music composition book, and begin.

The title is the easy part: *When Winter Robeson Came.*

Author's Note

AUGUST 1965 LEFT ME with some very vivid memories of the Watts Rebellion. Those six days were tumultuous and uncertain.

I remember my older brother and me standing side by side on the front porch of our house on 103rd Street, just west of Figueroa, not too far from Watts, watching as the National Guard patrolled our block. It was a Sunday. We were scared but, at the same time, intrigued. For days, we had not been allowed outside, but our curiosity won, and we snuck out because we just had to see. How much longer would it last? we wondered.

When Winter Robeson Came is fictional but told from the heart.

Acknowledgments

I am especially grateful to Nancy Paulsen for her editorial expertise, her guidance and patience as I plugged away at my first book in free verse, and for sharing my vision. A special thank-you to Sara LaFleur for everything she does. I would also like to express my gratitude to Mirelle Ortega for the wonderful artwork for the book jacket. An additional thank-you is sent to the copy editor, Ana Deboo, for her meticulous work. Of course, I am grateful to Penguin Random House for the publication of this novel and all those there, with jobs large and otherwise, who help bring the works of authors of color to the reading public. The stories of my people are plentiful.